Robinson
606 North Jefferson Street
Robinson, IL 62454-2699

DRUGS AND THE LAW

Police use modern equipment to monitor drunk drivers.

THE DRUG ABUSE PREVENTION LIBRARY

DRUGS AND THE LAW

Janet Grosshandler

Robinson Public Library District
606 North Jefferson Street
Robinson, IL 62454-2699

THE ROSEN PUBLISHING GROUP, INC.
NEW YORK

The people pictured in this book are only models; they, in no way, practice or endorse the activities illustrated. Captions serve only to explain the subjects of the photographs and do not imply a connection between the real-life models and the staged situations shown. News agency photographs are exceptions.

Published in 1993 by The Rosen Publishing Group, Inc.
29 East 21st Street, New York, NY 10010

Copyright 1993 by The Rosen Publishing Group, Inc.

All rights reserved. No part of this book may be reproduced in any form without permission in writing from the publisher, except by a reviewer.

First Edition

Manufactured in the United States of America

Library of Congress Cataloging-in-Publication Data

Grosshandler, Janet.
    Drugs and the law / by Janet Grosshandler.
      p. cm. — (The drug abuse prevention library)
    Includes bibliographical references and index.
    Summary: Discusses the different kinds of drugs and the American and international laws concerning their use.
        ISBN 0-8239-1463-1
        1. Drugs—Law and legislation—United States—Juvenile literature. 2. Narcotic laws—United States—Juvenile literature. 3. Drug abuse—United States—Prevention—Juvenile literature.
        [1. Narcotic laws. 2. Drug abuse.] I. Title. II. Series.
    KF3885.Z9G76   1993
    344.73'0446—dc 20
    [347304446]   92-33733
                                                                 CIP
                                                                   AC

Contents

	Introduction	6
Chapter 1	Tobacco Road	*11*
Chapter 2	Drinking and the Law	*19*
Chapter 3	Illegal Drugs	*27*
Chapter 4	New Drugs, New Laws	*39*
Chapter 5	Federal Drug Laws	*43*
Chapter 6	Out-of-Country Laws	*51*
Chapter 7	What You Can Do	*55*
	Help List	*59*
	Glossary—*Explaining New Words*	*60*
	For Further Reading	*62*
	Index	*63*

Introduction

"I just never thought I'd get caught," said Terry, 17, as he sat on his bed in the county juvenile shelter/jail. "Kirk asked me if I knew where to get some coke. I had some left over from the weekend, so I brought it to school and gave it to him. I didn't take any money, but here I am charged with being a dealer."

Terry's home state has strict laws about maintaining a "drug-free school zone." The law states that anyone convicted of passing a drug can be considered a dealer and therefore face going to prison without possibility of parole.

Arturo was only 18 when his nightmare began. A summer party seemed like a good idea after work on that lazy, hot day.

Introduction

The bash was going strong, but Arturo says he wasn't flat-out drunk—five beers over a few hours, no hard liquor.

On the way home from that party, Arturo hit a 23-year-old who was walking on the side of the road.

At the police station, Arturo was given an intoxilizer test. The test showed that his BAC (blood alcohol content) was .14, and he was arrested for DUI (driving under the influence).

Arturo was fingerprinted and spent the night in jail. His lawyer helped him get

Alcohol may impair driving skills and put other people at risk.

out on bail, but his troubles were only starting. The person he hit died. The charges against Arturo now included manslaughter.

"My friend and I were going to this party, and we got stopped by the cops for shooting through a yellow light turning red," said Kim, 16. "They searched the car and our stuff and found the little bit of pot I had in my pocketbook. It wasn't much, but they took us to the police station."

Under the law in Kim's state, anyone convicted of any drug offense loses his or her license for six months. Because she was under 17, the legal driving age, Kim lost the right to have a license for six months after she turned 17.

"I waited so long for my license, and now that I'm almost there I have to wait another six months!"

Substance-abuse laws are virtually everywhere—in every state in the U.S. and in other countries too. Laws against using, abusing, selling, distributing, and making drugs have been around for years, even hundreds of years.

In 1679 the colony of Massachusetts passed an antidrinking law because drunkenness was an "evil practice." In 1919 the 18th Amendment was added to the Constitution, outlawing beer, wine, and liquor in the United States. This was known as "Prohibition." It turned out to be the start of illegal activities by people who tried to outwit the law.

Tobacco has always been involved in American life. It is a commodity in our country's economic balance. Now laws regulate where people may smoke and where they may not and what kind of advertising tobacco companies are allowed to use. These laws have come about because of medical proof that tobacco products (cigarettes, cigars, chewing or smokeless tobacco) are responsible for heart disease and cancer.

We have thousands and thousands of laws. Senators, Congresspersons, mayors, town councils, school systems, and other officials make laws. The aim of the laws is generally to keep people safe and alive, to keep them from hurting one another or taking what is not rightfully theirs. Some people think we have too many laws; others think we don't have enough. In this book you'll be able to examine the impact that drugs have on our lives and the laws intended to keep us safe and alive when faced with illegal drugs or the misuse and abuse of drugs.

Store owners are required by law to check the age of young people buying cigarettes or alcohol.

CHAPTER 1

Tobacco Road

"I can go into this one store," said Tanya, 15, "and buy a pack of cigarettes, no problem. Then I'll go into another store, and they point to a sign that says it's illegal to sell cigarettes to anyone under 18. If we want them, we know where to get them."

There are laws that set fines for selling cigarettes to those under 18 years old. Enforcing the laws is not always easy, so the police and the courts rely on citizens to obey the laws. Some people will always try to get around the laws, thinking they won't be caught. The laws are made to protect people.

The laws restricting use of tobacco by minors (those under 18 years old) or forbidding smoking in public buildings are intended to help people. Tobacco contains the most addictive drug in America today. That drug is *nicotine*.

Nicotine is the poisonous ingredient in tobacco that causes addiction to cigarettes by people of all ages, even as young as eight or nine. It can act as a stimulant (speeding up your nervous system) or a depressant (slowing it down). The craving for nicotine becomes even stronger in addicts, and many people smoke two or three packs of cigarettes a day.

Smoking has been linked to cancer, heart and circulatory problems, and lung ailments. Chronic smokers suffer from coughs, emphysema, bronchitis, and other respiratory problems.

"Well, if someone wants to smoke," said Kate, 16, "isn't it their choice? They are the ones who suffer."

Kate asked the question that many smokers ask. Why interfere in my life? It's a free country, right?

Yes, the United States does guarantee many freedoms. But medical research has shown that smoking is very dangerous to your health. Secondhand smoke for nonsmokers is also dangerous, and now laws protect those people too.

"I wish I had known how dangerous it was back when I started smoking 40 years ago," said Harry, 54. "We never knew. I never thought this could happen to me."

Harry has had part of one lung removed because of lung cancer caused by his smoking, yet when he left the hospital the first thing he did was light a cigarette.

There were laws against the use of tobacco as far back as 1604, when King James I of England denounced tobacco as harmful. More laws came from popes and rulers around the world.

As rolled cigarettes became available in America in the early 1900s, women and children soon took up the habit. Laws had been passed in 14 states by 1921, but they failed to stop people from smoking, and they were repealed.

In 1964 the Surgeon General of the United States made it official that cigarette smoking is a factor contributing to lung cancer. Despite warnings on cigarette packages, people continued to smoke.

"My father says that's when he quit," said Paul, 14. "He didn't like the idea that whenever he lit up he was lighting up a 'cancer stick'."

A long time ago, cigarette smoking was advertised as something healthy! Camel

Advertisements can make smoking look glamorous.

cigarettes had an ad that told people to smoke during their meal at Thanksgiving because it would help digest their food.

"Well, look at ads today," said Jemal, 14. "In magazines it looks like smoking makes you real cool, especially with girls. I look at my friends when they smoke, and they look kind of grown-up."

That's what the advertising companies want you to think. They are paid to sell a product. Famous people have endorsed their favorite cigarettes, including Ronald Reagan, who starred in ads for cigars also. Radio and television commercials painted visual pictures of how wonderful and attractive smoking was.

Until 1970, that is. As a result of the Surgeon General's report and the growing antismoking concerns, Congress passed a law forbidding the advertising of cigarettes on radio and TV after January 1, 1971.

Laws have been introduced on several occasions to ban cigarette advertising in magazines and on billboards. But they have failed to pass. The debate goes on whether advertising is protected under the First Amendment right to free speech or whether it is misleading and is therefore not protected by the Amendment.

"I think the strongest advertisement is that a lot of my friends smoke," said Jay, 15. "I don't have to look at ads. They tell me which ones they tried and offer me some. That's how I got started."

Encouragement by your friends isn't covered by any laws. You have to use your own mind and make this important decision for yourself. You might want to think about how your best friend's grandfather suffered and then died from lung cancer after smoking two packs of cigarettes a day for forty years. That may be the advertising that will influence your decision.

One way that the government is putting more pressure on people not to smoke is by taxing the purchase of cigarettes. Laws have been passed in many states banning the sale of tobacco products to anyone under 18 and fining those who are caught selling them.

"The best laws," commented Reba, 16, "have been the ones against smoking in restaurants and other places. I remember standing in the check-out line when we went grocery shopping, and this lady stood behind us and smoked. I was coughing all over the place because I couldn't move away from her, and the smoke was going

Many restaurants and other public places prohibit smoking in designated areas.

all over our food. She let the ash on her cigarette get real long, and it blew on the fruit in our basket. I had to wash my apple for a long time before I could get that smell off of it.

"Plus I thought of that ash having been in her mouth, which seemed pretty dirty to me because she was coughing too, and now it was on the skin of my apple that I was going to put in my mouth. Yuck!"

Because of new information and a growing interest in health and fitness, the number of smokers today has dropped. Surveys show that teenage smoking has slowed down over the past 15 years, although teenage girls still smoke more than boys.

The American Cancer Society hopes that by the year 2000 everyone can be living in a "smoke-free society."

"I don't know if smoking will ever disappear totally," said Zoe, 15. "On one hand so many laws are being made, I don't know if they can all be enforced. On the other hand it seems as if people do care about other people's health, you know? I mean, I wish I could get Mom to quit. I hate it. But she doesn't break any laws with her smoking. Sometimes it takes more than laws, I guess."

CHAPTER 2

Drinking and the Law

"I'm eighteen," Malcolm said. "I can vote. I can get married. I can be a father. I can join the Army and fight and possibly be killed for my country. I can get a loan. I can get insurance. I am an adult. Then why is it illegal for me to drink?"

Malcolm's question has been going the seesaw route for many years now. After Prohibition was repealed in 1933 and the sale of alcohol was legal again, and after the Vietnam War, the debate over lowering the drinking age came up again. After 1972, when the legal voting age was lowered to 18, the legal drinking age was lowered in several states.

Over the next ten years, however, more and more teenagers were drinking.

Sixteen- and 17-year-olds bought liquor with false identification. Alcoholism increased among teenagers, and so did motor vehicle accidents caused by drinking and driving.

Seeing what was happening to the teenagers in America, many people began to push for raising the drinking age again. Since 1980 most of the states have set the legal drinking age at 21. Even though it is illegal to buy and drink alcohol, however, teenagers who drink and drive are still causing serious problems.

Statistics show that more than half of the deaths on the nation's roads involve alcohol. And 1 in every 15 high school seniors drinks alcohol "frequently." Drunk driving causes the greatest number of deaths in the 15- to 24-year-old group. Every 20 minutes an American is killed in an alcohol-related car accident, and teens are involved more than any other age group.

If you or a friend with whom you are driving are pulled over on the suspicion of DUI, you'll be asked to take a breath test to determine the level of alcohol in your body. If you refuse or fail the test, your driver's license is taken away for thirty days or more.

Police have the right to give a "breath test" if they suspect someone of drunk driving.

You may think that's not fair. If you refuse the test, you are presumed guilty, so you have to take the test to prove you are innocent. Maybe you think that is losing your freedom, but when you drive a car drunk, you are driving what could be a deadly weapon. Taking another's life is taking his or her most precious freedom.

When you drink and drive you gamble on being arrested, failing the intoxication tests, going to jail, hiring a lawyer, going to court, being sentenced, and paying a fine. You lose. And so do other people.

CONVICTION: If you are found guilty of DUI, the judge may sentence you to jail for days, weeks, or months.

DUI is a criminal offense.

FINES: DUI fines vary among the states, but you may pay from $250 to $1,000 for your first conviction.

JAIL: You might be sentenced to 48 hours or up to a year in jail for DUI. Some judges will allow you to do community service instead of jail time.

REHABILITATION: DUI offenders usually have to go through a driver improvement program. You may be required to undergo an alcohol recovery program.

PROBATION: Some states require probation after a jail sentence or in place of it. That means that the way you live and behave will be checked on over a period of time, possibly one to three years. Your probation officer will check with your family, school, employer, teachers, and others to make sure you are staying out of trouble.

LICENSE REVOCATION: The privilege of driving (remember how long you waited for that) is taken away. If you get a DUI conviction, you can kiss your license goodbye for quite a while.

You can find out about your state's DUI law at the police department in your town or the county judge's office. When you take driver education class in high school (which is required in most school systems), the law is spelled out for you. Make sure you pay attention to it.

Some states now have host-liability laws too. These make you responsible if something happens. If you have a party at your house and you are under 18, your parents are liable if anything goes wrong. If a friend leaves your party drunk, tries to drive, and has an accident, your parents could be sued for damages.

Parties can be fun without alcohol.

Serving alcohol to minors is restricted by laws as well. If you are 18 or 19 and you give or serve alcohol to a minor, you could be arrested and fined. YOU are liable.

Because of these laws and the number of Americans who are now concerned, the fatal-accident statistics are going down. Studies show that more teens are aware and are slowing down on drinking and on drinking and driving. It's okay to take your own six-pack of soda, instead of beer, to a party. More kids are saying no to getting into a car when a friend who has been drinking wants to drive.

These laws are passed as protection for people—especially innocent people. Recently in New Jersey a young mother and her four-month-old baby were killed in the backseat of their car when a drunk driver plowed into it. The young father and son who were in the front seat were injured. Four lives shattered. The drunk driver was not badly hurt. He is now serving time in jail.

"Some kids say that if they want to drink, it's their business," said Sasha, 17. "I say no way, buddy. It's my business too. If you plow into my car or drive me off the road, it is *my* business too. It's my *life!*"

Many drugs are made in illegal labs.

CHAPTER 3

Illegal Drugs

Cocaine, marijuana, heroin, and other drugs are governed all over the country by both federal and state laws. These drugs were not always considered illegal. One hundred years ago some of them were made, advertised, and sold as "elixirs," or medicines. People drank coca wine, which contained cocaine, to relax and "cure" their day-to-day ailments.

Coca-Cola, created in 1886 by Dr. J.C. Pemberton, was said to be a nonalcoholic drink. The ingredients included cola nuts, caramel, and coca leaves (cocaine). In 1903 cocaine was removed from the drink, and caffeine was substituted for it.

Opium and morphine, an ingredient of opium, were used widely in the late 1800s.

Used as a painkiller, morphine could be found in many medicines that were available to anyone.

Americans were becoming addicted to these drugs. The "cure-all" claims of the elixirs were discovered to be untrue, and a reform movement began. President Theodore Roosevelt and the Congress passed the Pure Food and Drug Act of 1906, which began government control and regulation of drugs. Labels had to state how much morphine or other drug was in a particular medicine.

Opium use was becoming a worldwide problem. President Roosevelt took part in an international conference in 1909 to discuss various solutions. In 1911 a second conference passed The Hague International Opium Convention, which tried to control the making and selling of these drugs all over the world.

The United States in 1914 passed the Harrison Narcotic Act, which was the first law in America intended to control the use of drugs.

What's the big deal about all these facts? you might ask. What's it got to do with me?

Looking back over the years, it helps to see that there have always been people

The U.S. Coast Guard seizes illegal drugs.

who cared about other people. That's the main reason for making laws—to keep people safe and healthy.

Another reason is to make you aware of what happens to you when you break the laws—the consequences and penalties. It is even written into some laws that you cannot use the "I-didn't-know" argument as a defense.

Terry Farley, a county prosecutor in New Jersey, says, "The law pretty much says that if you are 18 or 80, if you deal drugs and do not cooperate, you are going to jail." Even if you are 16 or 17 you can be tried as an adult in criminal court and face adult sentences.

If you are tried as a juvenile, however, the judge has some leeway in deciding your punishment. Often judges will send kids to drug and alcohol rehabilitation programs as part of their sentence.

"I was in the juvenile shelter," said Frank, 14. "That's like kids' jail. I was caught with some crack, and the judge talked to me a long time about doing drugs. He said he could sentence me to do time or I could go to a rehab. I decided to do the rehab. One of my friends took rehab as a way to get out of jail, but he's back in already. He didn't take it seriously.

Illegal Drugs

These young men have taken the first courageous step toward recovery by joining this rehabilitation group in Queens, New York.

DRUGS AND THE LAW

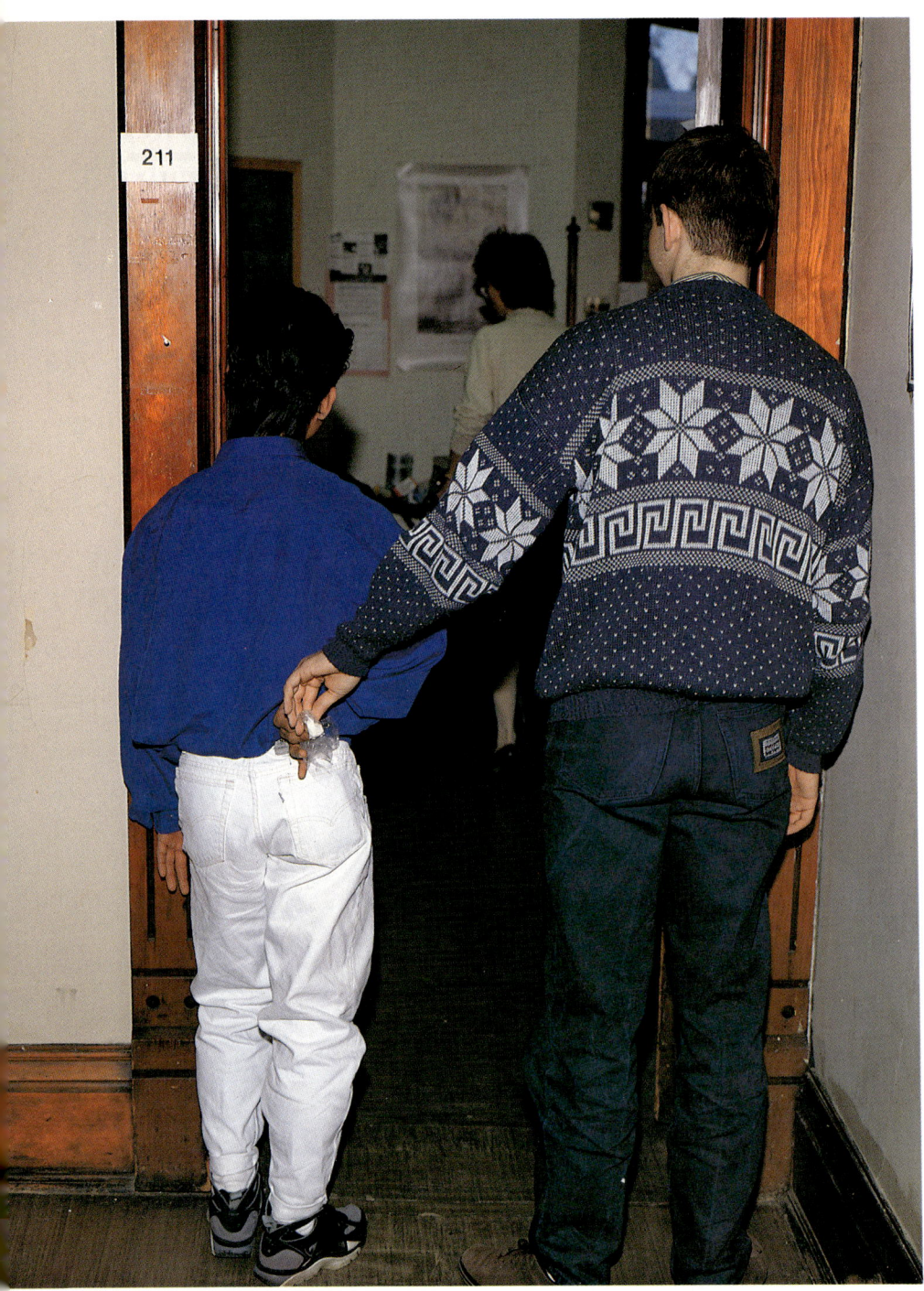

It is illegal to distribute drugs even if no money is exchanged.

I think I will. I don't want to be back here or go to jail for six months or a year."

Prosecutor Farley says, "When I go around to the schools and talk to kids about the law, I tell them that if they're under 18, the juvenile system won't be as tough. You'll get a chance to clean up your act. But once you're over 18, if you keep doing it—then watch out. We'll come down hard."

Laws differ around the country, but most laws have more similarities than differences. The federal Food and Drug Act defines what categories the various drugs fall into, and the states write laws depending on how dangerous the drug is and how much of the drug a person possesses or tries to distribute.

"Distribute" does not always mean to sell the drug. It can mean giving or passing or attempting to transfer drugs to another person. No money has to change hands for you to be arrested and convicted for distributing. If you are over 18 and distribute drugs to anyone under that age, you can be subject to twice the term of imprisonment, fine, or other penalty in some states.

"Controlled dangerous substances" are organized into separate categories or "schedules." Depending on what you do with any of these drugs, you may face first-degree, second-degree, third-degree, or fourth-degree charges. For example, possessing five ounces or more of heroin or cocaine may be a special first-degree crime and bring you 15 years in state prison even if it's your first offense.

The categories or schedules of drugs are based on how medically dangerous a drug is in its effects. Schedule I or Category I usually includes opiates, heroin, LSD, morphine, codeine compounds, and amphetamines. Schedules II, III, and IV may be third-degree crimes. The fines for possessing or distributing may be up to $25,000, plus a jail term.

Having small amounts of marijuana (pot, grass, etc.) or very small amounts of hashish ("hash") may bring 100 or more hours of community service. You may have to clean up litter on your town's roads and highways, or you may have to paint the community center.

In many states, if you are convicted of any drug crime you forfeit (give up, lose) your driver's license for six months or as long as two years. So the privilege of driving is lost too when you are found guilty of breaking the drug laws.

There are even stricter laws concerning drugs. If someone dies as a result of your giving him or her drugs, you can be tried and convicted of the first-degree crime of homicide (the killing of a human being). You will be charged with a major crime if you distribute or dispense a controlled dangerous substance in Schedule I or II that causes the death of another.

Most of the states (45 at present) have laws about "drug-free school zones." The penalty for breaking the "safety zone" is a minimum prison term of three years, possibly without any time off for good behavior. Small amounts of marijuana or hashish usually carry a one-year term.

"School property" means any public, private, or parochial school. The limit is 1,000 feet from the school property, not just the school building.

Protection of children and teenagers is the idea behind this law. State laws are becoming stricter and tougher on drug dealing and possession because too many lives have been ruined by drugs. People care and want to keep others safe and off drugs. That's why laws are made and enforced.

Here is an interesting result of a drug law. A 15-year-old from Massachusetts,

Sean Cann, had little trouble buying cigarettes from a store. He was refused only twice over three years because he was under the legal age to buy them. Now, six years later, the lawsuit that Sean filed has been settled.

Sean and another person sued the store that illegally sold them cigarettes for those three years. The lawsuit stated that the store was responsible for their nicotine addiction. As part of the settlement, the store has agreed to check carefully the age of young people trying to buy cigarettes and even to require proof.

The law is being enforced more strictly because of the lawsuit. Stores are taking it upon themselves to enforce the law because they don't want to get caught up in a legal battle.

Similar laws exist in 45 states and Washington, D.C. Because so many stores sell cigarettes, they are not easy to enforce. Antismoking groups have pushed for these laws. Statistics show that 90 percent of Americans who smoke started before the age of 21. So if more preteens and teenagers find it hard to buy cigarettes, maybe they won't start.

These are not the only laws designed to stop young people from smoking. Utah has banned vending machines; you can buy cigarettes only in stores, where they can check your age. The cities of Chicago, New York, and Washington have issued this ban too.

Seventeen states have laws by which underage teenagers and preteens are fined for possession of tobacco. Under a brand-new law passed in New Hampshire, young people under 18 years old can be fined $25 if they are found "using, purchasing, or possessing tobacco."

Hey, you might say, what ever happened to freedom of choice? Isn't this America? Yes, it is America, and in this country a lot of studies have been done on smoking. Did you know that nicotine addiction is usually the first drug addiction people acquire?

So the idea is to keep you alive.

All these laws concerning drugs and drinking/drugging and driving are there for your protection and the protection of innocent people whom you might involve in your drug use. Many people go through their whole lives without ever worrying about being caught with drugs. They just don't start using.

Athletes should never use drugs to build muscles or to increase strength. Excellent physical condition is a result of steady work and discipline.

CHAPTER 4

New Drugs, New Laws

National Football League star Lyle Alzado's life is a mess from using them.

World-class sprinter and track star Ben Johnson lost two years of his running career to them.

Some athletes use and abuse them.

What are they?

They are anabolic steroids. These drugs were developed during the 1930s to build body tissue and to stop such tissue from deteriorating (breaking down) from illness or disease.

Today anabolic steroids are used and abused by young athletes trying to build bigger muscles. Both males and females are involved. They are in high school, in college, and in professional sports and body-building programs.

Steroids have a long list of dangerous or life-threatening side effects:

- cancer
- acne
- liver disease and tumors
- heart disease
- kidney disease and kidney stones
- high blood pressure
- fever
- diarrhea
- headaches
- nausea or vomiting
- stunted growth in teenagers
- aggressive and violent behavior
- mood swings
- psychological addiction
- blood poisoning from injections
- vomiting blood
- liver-kidney failure
- death

A new federal law has been passed to combat these dangerous drugs. The Anabolic Steroids Control Act of 1990 makes it a crime for anyone to possess, prescribe, or distribute anabolic steroids for use in humans other than in treating disease or other medical conditions.

The penalty for the distribution of or the prescription of steroids may be a prison sentence of up to five years and a fine of up to $250,000 for a first offense. A second offense can bring a prison sentence of up to ten years and a fine of up to $500,000.

If you are using steroids, be warned—you could be pumping iron behind bars. Possession and use of these drugs is a fourth-degree crime and carries a prison sentence of up to 18 months. Possession with intent to distribute is a third-degree crime and can bring a sentence of three to five years.

If these penalties sound severe, consider this:

John was 23 years old. A bodybuilder, he had been using anabolic steroids to "bulk up." He was proud of his body. On the outside it looked extremely strong and muscular.

But the steroid use was too much for the inside of his body. Late one night he was admitted to the hospital. Doctors were forced to put him directly into the intensive care unit. His liver and his kidneys, which process and cleanse the blood, had failed, shut down. The doctors hooked him up to machines that would perform the functions that his own organs could no longer do. The steroids had robbed him of his power.

Four days later John suffered cardiac arrest (heart failure) and died. When the autopsy was performed, even more damage was discovered. The steroids had caused the death of his liver tissue, and John had experienced complete kidney shutdown. His sexual organs had been damaged, and he was sterile, unable ever to father a child had he lived.

Laws are made to protect people. Perhaps if his drug pusher (supplier) had been caught and arrested, John would have lived. Perhaps if he had been found and charged with possession, he might have lived. Perhaps if he had never started, he'd be alive today.

As new drugs surface, new laws are passed to combat their use. Freebase cocaine, better known as "crack," hit the streets some years ago, and police and government officials work hard to counteract the growing addiction, health problems, and crime that crack brings with it.

Laws will continue to be passed and enforced as long as drugs are on the streets and in the hands of Americans.

CHAPTER 5

Federal Drug Laws

Over the years the federal government has passed several laws to control the manufacture, distribution, and use of many drugs.

The first law passed by Congress was the Harrison Narcotic Act of 1914, and its purpose was to control the use of drugs. In 1924 the use of heroin was becoming a big problem, and it was not covered under the Harrison Act. So in 1924 the Harrison Act was expanded to include heroin on the list of forbidden drugs.

Over the next forty years or so Congress passed some 55 laws to make the Harrison Act stronger. Punishments and penalties for breaking these laws were increased, and new drugs such as LSD and PCP ("angel dust") were banned also.

In 1970 the Comprehensive Drug Abuse Prevention and Control Act brought all the drug laws under one act. It was this law that set up the categories or schedules of drugs.

Schedule I drugs include those that have no use as medicine and cause strong addiction and abuse. Schedule II drugs are those drugs that have some value as medicine, such as morphine and codeine, as well as cocaine. Schedule III drugs are those that may be prescribed by a doctor and are not so potentially addicting. Schedule IV drugs include painkillers, Valium, and others. Schedule V drugs are medications that contain a small quantity of a drug, such as a cough medicine with codeine or something with a small amount of a narcotic.

Antidrug organizations that are part of the federal government include the Drug Enforcement Administration, the Federal Bureau of Investigation (FBI), the Coast Guard, the Bureau of Customs (which inspects luggage, packages, and people coming into this country), and the Bureau of Alcohol, Tobacco, and Firearms. These and other organizations work at our

Dealing drugs in school zones results in severe penalties.

country's borders, around the United States, and around the world to enforce drug laws.

Government agents, marshals, CIA officials, and military people work to stop drugs from being smuggled into the country, where they may be sold.

The Anti-Drug Abuse Act of 1986 made the 1970 Act even stronger. It kept the same schedules of abused drugs but increased the penalties and punishments for possessing, distributing, and selling them. It also eliminated most of the suspended sentences or probation for drug abuse.

These federal laws give states, counties, and towns the authority to enforce local laws. School systems can enforce rules against drug abuse. Forty-five states now have drug-free school zone laws providing harsh penalties for possessing, using, or distributing drugs within a certain area around a school.

"We went on a school trip with our teachers," said Ross, 17. "Two kids were saying that they were bringing some dope. They didn't make any secret about it. Most of us who were going got the word.

"A few of us were annoyed. This was a cool trip, and here were these kids bringing the stuff and maybe ruining it for the rest of us. I thought about the whole bunch of us kids getting into trouble and maybe getting suspended from school or something.

"But these two kids talked so much that it got back to the teachers fast. They searched their stuff and found it. The last I heard they were still suspended, facing police charges, especially with that school zone law, and having to go in front of the school board. They might even be thrown out of school. What a way to end your school years!"

The federal government also becomes involved in drug laws when decisions must be made in a trial. When someone is convicted of a crime, an appeal can be made for a new trial based on additional evidence or the possibility of a reversal of the sentence. The Supreme Court, the highest court in the United States, hears cases that have been appealed from lower courts.

In a case in 1991 the Supreme Court ruled that the Constitution does allow a sentence of life in prison without parole for nonviolent first offenses, including possession of 1.5 pounds or more of cocaine. A man had been sentenced in

DRUGS AND THE LAW

48 the state of Michigan after being found guilty of having two pounds of cocaine in his possession. The defendant's lawyer argued that the sentence was too harsh for the crime committed, that other states did not impose such harsh sentences.

So the U.S. Supreme Court has to make decisions about drug laws based on the freedoms guaranteed in the Constitution. Federal courts have had to rule on the

Drug education starts in the early grades. Here, elementary school children hold up posters they created to promote safe driving.

drug laws enforced in schools. Drug policies in school systems usually include searches and urinalysis (testing the urine for the presence of drugs). The courts have had to rule whether these measures are legal.

According to federal and state laws, students who might be suspended or expelled from school for drug offenses must have warning in advance. Federal courts have ruled that a student must receive written notice of drug charges, a list of witnesses, and a chance to defend himself or herself.

When people feel that the government is too much involved in their lives, they say, "Big Brother is watching." The saying comes from the book *1984* by George Orwell, in which the government watched just about every action of the people. But the government works hard to make sure that each and every person accused of a drug crime receives all the rights and freedoms guaranteed by the Constitution.

Being accused, arrested, and convicted of a drug crime can affect the rest of your life. You have the choices before you. You are aware of the laws and the penalties. You control your life. Don't let drugs control it for you.

Drug enforcement may often be more strict outside the United States.

CHAPTER 6

Out-of-Country Laws

"**M**y dad and I were talking about getting caught with drugs in Canada or Mexico," said Juan, 17. "I didn't think laws were as strict as they are here in the United States. Then he made me watch the movie 'Midnight Express.' Even though it was a long time ago, it scared me."

Midnight Express is a book, with a movie made from it, about what happened to an American who tried to smuggle four pounds of hashish out of Turkey. In 1970, Billy Hayes wanted to bring the hash into the U.S. As he boarded the plane that would take him from Istanbul to New

York, the Turkish police arrested him after finding the drugs taped to his body.

Billy Hayes was sentenced to 30 years in prison. He was beaten, tortured, and lived in constant fear. After five years he escaped and made his way to Greece.

Other countries have stricter laws than America does. However, the U.S. does have agreements with some countries that allow American prisoners to come home and finish their sentence in an American prison.

Even famous people can wind up in prison because of drugs. Stacy Keach, an American actor from the old "Mike Hammer" series, was arrested in England in 1985 for trying to take almost $4,000 worth of cocaine out of that country. He served six months in jail there.

Paul McCartney, former Beatle of the 1960s who now plays with his own Wings band, was arrested in Japan in 1980 for possession of marijuana. The Japanese penalty for that offense is five years in prison. McCartney spent a week in jail and was required to leave the country. All his concerts were canceled.

Laws differ all over the world. Drunk driving may bring a sentence of two years in one country and ten years in another.

Some countries have specific laws for cocaine, heroin, marijuana, and the drugs made from them, but they may place others into categories of "dangerous drugs" or "morally offensive drugs."

In South Korea, Indonesia, and Malaysia you can be sentenced to death for dealing or selling "dangerous drugs" as well as heroin and cocaine. More than 50 countries have the same penalties for possession of an illegal drug and for selling or growing it. Just about 100 countries, including Mexico, Russia, France, Sweden, and Israel, have similar laws for all illegal substances.

What actually happens to you depends on the country's court system, judges, and prosecutors. Puffing some hash may get you fined and deported (sent back to America) or may land you in prison for several years.

In the U.S., if you are arrested, you are read your rights so that you know exactly what the charge is. You can call your lawyer or have one provided for you by the court. That is not always the case in other countries. If you are arrested for dealing or the possession of illegal substances, you may sit in jail for a month before you are even charged. The police may not call the

U.S. consul, your representative in a foreign country. If you do not speak the language, you may not be provided with an interpreter. Even if the consulate gets word to your family, there may not be much they can do except send you money for a lawyer or make sure you are treated decently.

In the U.S., if you are charged with a crime, you may be released from jail if you put up money for bail. In some countries there is no bail, so you sit in jail and wait.

All of these consequences are the result of choices you make. *You* take the risk when you break the law in this country or any country. If you choose to possess, give away, sell, or grow illegal drugs, you must be prepared to face the penalties.

A passport (your official identification as an American citizen, with your picture on it) will not get you out of trouble when you get yourself into trouble with drugs. The only way you can stay clear of drug arrest in a foreign country is not to possess, give away, or sell drugs. Stay clean, and you will stay out of jail.

CHAPTER 7

What You Can Do

When it comes to drugs and the law, it is important to know what's out there. Some teens really believe that "it could never happen to me." First and foremost, KEEP YOURSELF SAFE AND HEALTHY. Not getting involved with drugs in the first place is the goal. But many teens say, "It just happened. First a few beers and cigarettes, then some hard liquor. Pot came next and then someone had some coke, and so on and so on."

What seems simply innocent in the beginning—drinking a beer with some friends—can turn into a nightmare when you finish off the night in a car where the drinking/drugging driver crosses over the center line and crashes head-on into an innocent family coming home from the movies.

Staying straight when your friends are not may seem impossible at times. When you see them breaking laws and risking their freedom and their lives, you face some very hard decisions. Here are some teens who had to face tough situations.

Trevor, 18, knew that his girlfriend was going out with some kids who were heavily into experimenting.

"Kari was doing that stuff more and more, and she wanted me to do it with her.

"I admit that I scored some grass and used fake ID to buy stuff at the liquor store. And I drove high sometimes. I just didn't get caught. But the cocaine scared me. Kari would say that if I didn't get it for her, she'd get it herself.

"My older brother was on my back to get out of it. Plus I'm 18. I could have gone to jail for breaking lots of laws. It bothered me, but I figured Kari was worth it. But when she started with crack, I knew I couldn't go on.

"I went to her mom and told her that I was afraid that Kari was getting really messed up. She was skipping school, and her grades were bad. Her mom knew Kari was in trouble, but I guess when I told her all of it, she got scared. Kari's parents got her into a rehab.

"When she came back, she said her drug problems were partly my fault, so she wouldn't go out with me.

"I'm sorry for us, for Kari. I think we got too wrapped up in getting high. We just didn't think. I guess I'm lucky. And maybe Kari is too. But it still hurts. We lost a lot because of drugs."

Trevor made decisions and took action to help himself and Kari before things were beyond help. Cherise wishes she had made a different decision.

"I knew my brother was into drugs. He would threaten me about not telling Dad. I knew he was dealing. I knew he was breaking laws. I stayed out of it.

"It was all over school about this big party weekend. There were going to be a couple of kegs. Then the stories started that you could get any drug you wanted there too—speed, pot, coke, acid—and my brother was the one getting all the stuff.

"When I heard about this party and what was going down, I was so mad! I wanted to tell Dad, especially when I heard that the police might pull a bust, but I didn't.

"Well, the police did come and my brother was arrested. He was charged with dealing, distributing to minors, and a few other things. Then you know what? Dad got mad at me because I knew and didn't tell on him. My brother is waiting for sentencing; his life is a mess. Dad's mad at him and mad at me, and we're all miserable."

To tell or not to tell. Many times that is the question. Do you tell on your best friend and get him "in trouble"? What's friendship worth?

These are decisions and situations you may face in the next few years.

There are people to whom you can talk. In your school a trusted teacher, guidance counselor, class advisor, or substance-abuse counselor can help you.

Talking to your friend's parents, brothers, sisters, or best friends can also be a way to go. Letting someone know that trouble can be coming may save a life and help prevent a tragedy.

You are not in this world alone. Protect yourself by living within the law and helping others to do that too.

Stay safe, straight, and alive. The world is a wonderful place to live.

Help List

Alcoholics Anonymous World Services, Inc.
P.O. Box 459
Grand Central Station
New York, New York, 10163

MADD
Mothers Against Drunk Driving
669 Airport Freeway, Suite 310
Hurst, Texas, 76053

Narcotics Anonymous World Service Office
16155 Wyandotte Street
Van Nuys, CA 91406

National Council on Alcoholism
1-800-662-2255

National Highway Traffic and Safety Administration
400 Seventh Street SW
Washington, D.C. 20590

National Institute on Drug Abuse
1-800-662-HELP

Places to Contact for Information
Police department (local, county, and state)
Court system (local, county, and state)
Lawyers' offices
Law libraries

Glossary
Explaining New Words

addiction A habit so strong that a person cannot give it up; it may be physically or emotionally based.

alcoholism An illness in which there is a strong desire to continue drinking alcoholic liquor.

anabolic steroids Drugs developed in the 1930s to build body tissue and stop diseased tissue from breaking down.

autopsy Examination of a dead body to find the cause of death.

BAC (blood alcohol content) Measurement of the amount of alcohol in the bloodstream found by taking a blood sample.

bail Money left with a court as a guarantee that an arrested person will appear for trial.

commodity Anything that is bought or sold.

consequence A result or an outcome.

conviction Being found guilty of a crime.

DUI (driving under the influence) Operating a motor vehicle while using drugs, including alcohol.

enforce To make people obey.

illegal Not allowed by law.

intoxilizer test Breath test used by police to determine the level of alcohol in a person's blood.

juvenile Under most laws, a person not yet 18 years old.

liability Obligation by law to be responsible.

parole Being allowed to go free before a full prison sentence has been served.

possession The act of holding or owning something.

probation Release from prison under the supervision of a court officer.

rehabilitation Restoration to a normal and good condition; in the case of drugs, a supervised program where one can return to a sober, straight life-style.

revoke To put an end to, as a law, license, or permit.

urinalysis Test of a person's urine for the presence of drugs.

For Further Reading

Dolan, Edward F., Jr. *International Drug Traffic*. New York: Franklin Watts, 1985.

Grauer, Neil A. *Encyclopedia of Psychoactive Drugs: Drugs and the Law*. New York: Chelsea House Publications, 1988.

Greenhouse, Linda. "Mandatory Life Term Is Upheld in Drug Case." *New York Times*, June 28, 1991.

Miller, Roger W. "Athletes and Steroids: Playing a Deadly Game." Project G.O.O.D., Ocean County, N.J., 1991.

New Jersey State Bar Association. "Legal Consequences of Substance Abuse." New Brunswick, N.J., 1989.

Snyder, Solomon, H. *Encyclopedia of Psychoactive Drugs: Drugs and Crime*. New York: Chelsea House Publications, 1988.

U.S. Department of Education. *What Works: Schools Without Drugs*. Washington, D.C.: Government Printing Office, 1986.

Index

A
alcohol, 7, 19, 20
   driving and, 7, 20, 21, 22–23, 25
   the law and, 7, 22–23, 25
   Massachusetts colony (1679) and, 8–9
   minors and, 19–20, 25
   statistics about, 20
alcoholism, 20
Alzado, Lyle, 39
American Cancer Society, 18
Anabolic Steroids Control Act of 1990, 40
Anti-Drug Abuse Act of 1986, 46

C
caffeine, 27
Coca-Cola, 27
Comprehensive Drug Abuse Prevention and Control Act of 1970, 44
Constitution (U.S.), 47, 48, 49
   amendments to, 8–9, 15

D
"drug-free school zones," 6, 35, 45, 46

drugs, 27, 34, 42, 43, 52, 53
   categories of, 33–34, 44, 53
   distribution of, 6, 30, 32, 33, 34, 35, 43
   federal organizations against, 29, 44, 46
   the law and, 9, 27, 30, 34–37, 53
   manufacture of, 43
   minors and, 30, 33, 56, 58
   schools and, 48–49

E
elixirs, 27, 28

H
Hague International Opium Convention, 28
Harrison Narcotic Act of 1914, 28, 43
   heroin and, 43
help, seeking, 58, 59

J
James I (king of England), 13
Johnson, Ben, 39

K
Keach, Stacy, 52

M
McCartney, Paul, 52
Midnight Express, 51–52
morphine, 27–28, 34, 44

O
opium, 27–28, 34
Orwell, George, 49

P
Pemberton, Dr. J.C., 27
Prohibition, 9, 19
Pure Food and Drug Act of 1906, 28

R
Reagan, Ronald, 15
rehabilitation programs, 22, 31
Roosevelt, Theodore, 28

S
steroids, anabolic, 39–40
    damages and side effects from, 40, 42
    distribution of, 41
    possession of, 41
Supreme Court (U.S.), 47–48

T
tobacco (smoking), 9, 10, 11–12
    advertising and, 13, 15, 16
    dangers of, 9, 12–13
    minors and, 11, 36–37
    nicotine in, 12
    secondhand smoke from, 12
    statistics about, 36
    taxes and, 16

V
Vietnam War, 19

About the Author
Janet Grosshandler is a guidance counselor at Jackson Memorial High School, Jackson, New Jersey.

She earned a B.A. at Trenton State College in New Jersey and followed soon after with an M.Ed. from Trenton while teaching seventh-grade English.

Janet lives in Jackson with her three sons, Nate, Jeff, and Mike.

Photo Credits
Cover: Stuart Rabinowitz.
Photos on pages 2, 48, 50: Wide World Photos; pp. 7, 45: Ned Gerard; pp. 10, 15, 38, 17, 24: Stuart Rabinowitz; p. 21: © Hemsey/Gamma-Liaison; p. 26: Gamma-Liason; p. 29: © L. Novovitch/Gamma-Liaison; p. 31: © Stephen Ferry/Gamma-Liaison.

Design & Production: Blackbirch Graphics, Inc.